An intriguing and delicious story that any child will love.

—Sharlyn Gerlinger,
First Grade Teacher

Our students were captivated by the pictures, humor, and hunger the story provoked.

—Marilyn Carsia and Sandra Valderaz,
Fifth Grade Teachers

This book is a charming an~~d~~ _____ ~~aining account of a true s~~t_____ ~~ef its of truly listening to y~~_____

—Rita Patzke,
Substitute Teacher

Published by Tate Publishing & Enterprises, LLC
127 E. Trade Center Terrace | Mustang, Oklahoma 73064 USA
1.888.361.9473 | www.tatepublishing.com

Tate Publishing is committed to excellence in the publishing industry. The company reflects the philosophy established by the founders, based on Psalm 68:11,
"The Lord gave the word and great was the company of those who published it."

Book design copyright © 2010 by Tate Publishing, LLC. All rights reserved.
Cover and Interior design by Michael Lee
Illustration by Kathy Hoyt

Published in the United States of America
ISBN: 978-1-61663-270-0
Juvenile Fiction: Humorous Stories
10.04.18

Paul and the
House Full of
Donuts

Starla Howard Davis

To: Ryder Russo, Enjoy your tasty treat! Starla Howard Davis

TATE PUBLISHING & *Enterprises*

I dedicate this book to my dad. I love to
hear his stories, especially the ones about
his childhood.

To my husband and my children, I love you.

To my parents, my sisters, my family, and to all my wonderful friends, thank you so much for being such a blessing in my life.

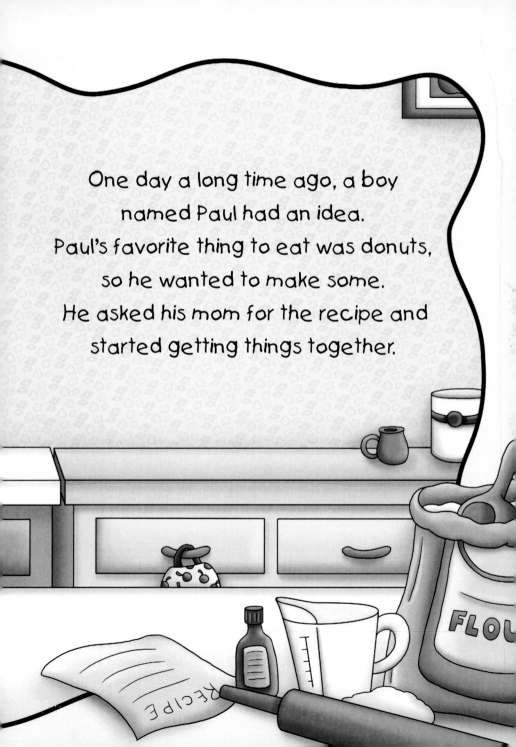

One day a long time ago, a boy
named Paul had an idea.
Paul's favorite thing to eat was donuts,
so he wanted to make some.
He asked his mom for the recipe and
started getting things together.

His mother told him,
"The recipe makes a lot.
Don't double the recipe!"

After she left, he decided to not just double the recipe, but to **quadruple** the recipe. That's four times as much!

When his mother came back,
she looked at Paul and said,
"Oh no! There are donuts everywhere!"

She was cross with Paul and told him,
"You have to finish cooking all
these donuts by yourself.
No one will help you!"

After hours of cooking, Paul was done.
Donuts were everywhere: in every
pot, pan, and dish in the house.
Even the bathtub was full of donuts!

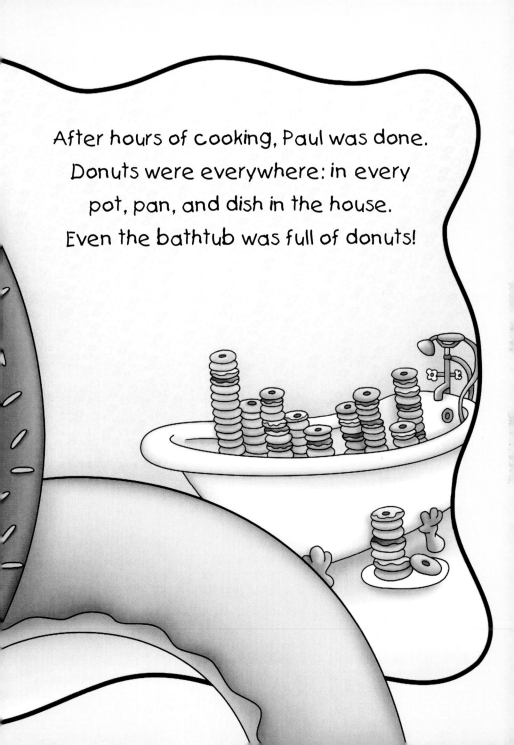

That night, Paul's mom came to say
prayers and say goodnight.
She said, "I guess you learned
a good lesson today."
Paul nodded. "Yes! Listen to your
mother...and make less donuts."

Note from the Author

This is a true story about my father. It happened back in the 1930's. He was about ten years old and lived on a farm with his parents, grandparents, five sisters and two brothers. Paul cooked so many donuts that they ate donuts for two weeks! He still loves donuts to this day.

AUDIO BOOK DOWNLOAD INCLUDED WITH THIS BOOK!

In your hands you hold a complete digital entertainment package. Besides purchasing the paper version of this book, this book includes a free download of the audio version of this book. Simply use the code listed below when visiting our website. Once downloaded to your computer, you can listen to the book through your computer's speakers, burn it to an audio CD or save the file to your portable music device (such as Apple's popular iPod) and listen on the go!

How to get your free audio book digital download:

1. Visit www.tatepublishing.com and click on the e|LIVE logo on the home page.
2. Enter the following coupon code:
   b150-a558-e2a7-bd10-46ce-8edd-8303-2208
3. Download the audio book from your e|LIVE digital locker and begin enjoying your new digital entertainment package today!